THE CURIOUS LITTLE KITTEN'S FIRST CHRISTMAS

By Linda Hayward
Illustrated by Maggie Swanson

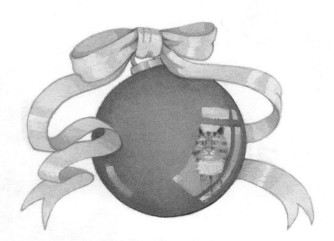

A GOLDEN BOOK · NEW YORK
Western Publishing Company, Inc., Racine, Wisconsin 53404

Copyright © 1984 by Linda Hayward. Illustrations copyright © 1984 by Maggie Swanson. All rights reserved. Printed in the U.S.A. No part of this book may be reproduced or copied in any form without written permission from the publisher. GOLDEN®, GOLDEN & DESIGN®, A FIRST LITTLE GOLDEN BOOK®, and A GOLDEN BOOK® are trademarks of Western Publishing Company, Inc. Library of Congress Catalog Card Number: 83-83293 ISBN 0-307-10127-4/ISBN 0-307-68151-3 (lib. bdg.)

G H I J

It was the night before Christmas.
Everyone in the house was asleep.
Everyone, that is, except a curious
little kitten.

She was wide awake—
and full of curiosity!

She was curious about the stockings
hanging by the fireplace.

She had seen stockings before, of course.
She had seen them in drawers—
                    and on people's feet.

She had seen stockings hanging on
the clothesline.

But she had never seen stockings
hanging by the fireplace. She wondered
and wondered—why were they there?

The little kitten was also curious about
the big green tree in the living room.

She had seen trees before, of course.
She had seen them in the back yard—

and in the front yard.

She had seen many, many trees in the park.

But she had never seen a tree in the
living room. She wondered and wondered—
what kind of tree was this?

The little kitten was especially curious about the things she saw on the tree. The trees outdoors were full of leaves.

This tree was full of balls and paper chains.

And here was something that made the little kitten more curious than ever. On the ledge beside the fireplace, there was a little gingerbread house.

She had seen houses before, of course.
She had seen a house made of logs—
and a house made of bricks.

She had even seen a little house
made of building blocks.

But she had never seen a little house
which smelled this good. She wondered
and wondered—who lived inside?

The curious little kitten decided
to wait on the ledge by the
fireplace to see who came out of
the gingerbread house.

It was a cozy and comfortable spot.
And even though the little kitten tried
and tried to stay awake, she fell asleep.
She slept for a long, long time.

When she woke up,
it was Christmas morning.
The little kitten was
so surprised.

The stockings were full of toys.
The floor under the big green tree was
covered with presents. And next to the
gingerbread house, there was a special
present just for her!

The little kitten wondered and wondered—
who filled the stockings and put the
presents under the tree? What was inside
all those packages?

Was the curious little kitten still curious?
Of course!